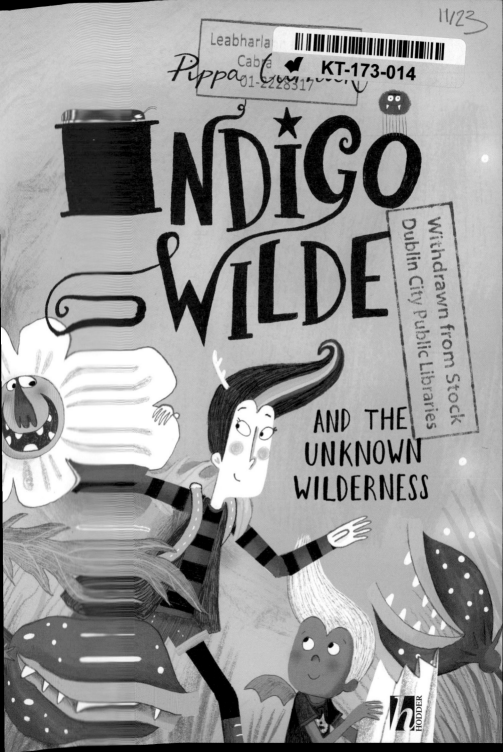

INDIGO WILDE

AND THE
UNKNOWN
WILDERNESS

Pippa Curnick

HODDER

HODDER CHILDREN'S BOOKS

First published in Great Britain in 2022 by Hodder & Stoughton
This paperback edition published in 2023

1 3 5 7 9 10 8 6 4 2

Text and illustrations copyright © Pippa Curnick, 2022

ISBN 978 1 444 948844

Printed and bound in China

The paper and board used in this book are made from wood from
responsible sources

MIX
Paper from
responsible sources
FSC® C169965

Hodder Children's Books
An imprint of Hachette Children's Group
Part of Hodder & Stoughton Limited
Carmelite House
50 Victoria Embankment
London EC4Y 0DZ
An Hachette UK Company
www.hachette.co.uk
www.hachettechildrens.co.uk

This book is dedicated to these exceptional explorers:

DR YETI: ALCHEMIST & FUEL CELL ENTHUSIAST

TIFFY: WEATHER-WITCH & MANATEENICORN AMBASSADOR

The Daily Waffle

SECRET NEWS FOR EXPLORERS OF UNKNOWN WORLDS
THURSDAY 8TH JULY

BETHESDA BROLLY, EXPLORER AND ADVENTURER, MISSING.

Miss Bethesda Brolly, of Shelton Lock, is the latest Explorer to vanish from the Jungliest Jungle of the Unknown Wilderness, in a series of mysterious disappearances.

Miss Brolly set off on a hike from her campsite last Wednesday, but has not been in contact with the Explorers' Council since.

A number of other Explorers have gone missing in the area in recent weeks. Bernhardt Abernathy, celebrated Inventor, and his wife, the Enchantress Cleopatra, disappeared without trace from the same campsite just two weeks ago, along with an injured unicorn they had been nursing back to health. Revered botanist, Professor Gazania Atakuma, vanished from a nearby glade where she had been collecting saliva samples from man-eating Belladonna plants. Tantalising reports of strange music being heard in the region may or may not be connected with these disturbing disappearances.

MISSING

BERNHARDT ABERNATHY

ENCHANTRESS CLEOPATRA

PROF. GAZANIA ATAKUMA

BETHESDA BROLLY

If you have any information regarding the whereabouts of Miss Brolly, Mr and Mrs Abernathy or Professor Atakuma, please call 0899-627-289 and quote reference:

FLIP FLOP CLIP CLOP WHIZZY WOZZY WOO.

–ONE–
THE DOORBELL, AGAIN

CLANG
CLANG

Indigo dropped the postcard she had been
reading in surprise and spilled her
mug of milkshake into her lap.
It was far too late to be the
milkman, or the postman.
Indigo gulped – the last
time the doorbell had
rung out of the blue,
the house had been
half destroyed by an

invisible, fire-breathing, chocolate-obsessed wabbit that her parents had sent them via Monster Mail. Indigo jumped up and signed to her little brother, Quigley, who was playing chess at the kitchen table with Queenie the goblin. Quigley had gone deaf as a baby, but the CLANGS of the rusty old doorbell still made him look up when they shook the chess pieces from the board.

Indigo pushed back the bolts and dragged the heavy front door open, feeling apprehensive, but a little bit excited, too. She wondered what sort of Creature her parents had sent this time …

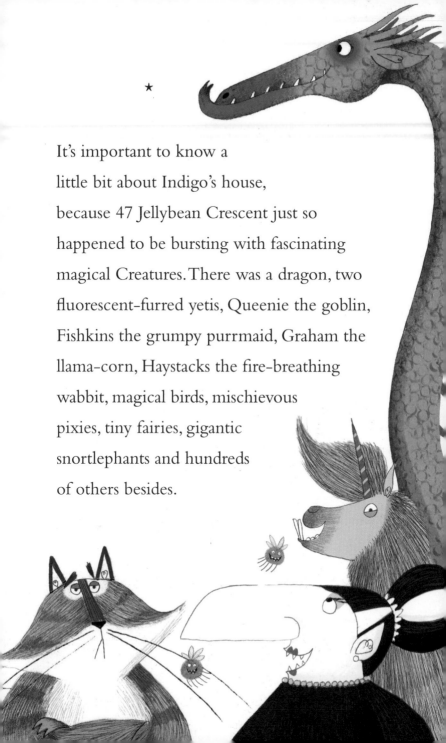

It's important to know a
little bit about Indigo's house,
because 47 Jellybean Crescent just so
happened to be bursting with fascinating
magical Creatures. There was a dragon, two
fluorescent-furred yetis, Queenie the goblin,
Fishkins the grumpy purrmaid, Graham the
llama-corn, Haystacks the fire-breathing
wabbit, magical birds, mischievous
pixies, tiny fairies, gigantic
snortlephants and hundreds
of others besides.

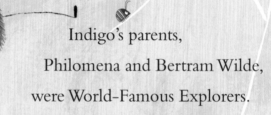

Indigo's parents,

Philomena and Bertram Wilde,

were World-Famous Explorers.

They had sent all of these spectacular

Creatures to the house (often without

warning) because the Creatures had been cast

out of their natural homes for being different

or unusual. Some only stayed for a little

while and some stayed for ever. If a Creature

arrived that needed a bit more room, the

house would just grow a new turret or tower

to accommodate. (On Tuesday, Mr and Mrs

Wilde had sent a crate of acrobatic spiders

the size of CARS and the house had grown an

entirely new amphitheatre on the

sixth floor for their rehearsals.)

You'd think the neighbours

on Jellybean Crescent would

notice a new turret popping

up on the house next door, or the fact there was a dragon sucking peppermints in the back garden … but no, they seemed totally oblivious to the strange goings on at number 47, and went about their normal, sensible lives without giving the magnificent house a second glance. This was very fortunate as Indigo's parents often warned her that most people these days didn't understand anything that was even slightly magical or unusual or different. Who knew what would happen if the other inhabitants of Jellybean Crescent discovered they had goblins and trolls living next door – they'd probably have them locked up … or worse.

The only neighbour that showed the slightest interest in the Wildes' house was Madam Grey from number 55 – the most boring beige house on the whole street. She was just about the nosiest person in the living universe and her suspicions about the goings-on at number 47 had grown since her last, disastrous visit. Indigo and Quigley had been worried that the Creatures would be discovered and sent packing, but Madam Grey had convinced herself that it had all just been a hallucination brought on by eating an out-of-date lasagne.

So it was with a mixture of excitement and uncertainty that Indigo cracked open the front door to see what Creature her parents might have sent this time. And, oh, WHAT A CREATURE IT WAS ...

-TWO-
CALLISTO

The gigantic Creature had shining silver claws and jet-black fur that twinkled and shimmered as though it had been dusted with starlight. Its face was bear-like and, indeed, it could have been mistaken for a bear, had it not been for the huge black feathered wings growing from its back, the twisting silver horns on its head, or the fact it was speaking in English.

"Indigo Wilde?" said the bear-Creature, poking her massive head into the hall and knocking a picture off the wall.

"Y–y–yes. That's me," Indigo replied, in shock. She had never seen anything like this Creature in her life, not even in the *Abracadarium* – the magical book handed down through generations of Wildes.

"And Quigley Wilde?" said the Creature, sounding desperate as she pushed her wet bear nose into Quigley's hair and gave a great sniff.

"Yes, that's me," signed Quigley, with a nervous look at Indigo.

"Who are—" Indigo started.

"No time, no time," said the bear. "Your parents are in GRAVE DANGER. Lost. Captured. Gone. They need help."

Queenie looked up from the chessboard as the yeti twins, Olli and Umpf, sloped into the room to listen. Graham the llama-corn bounced past the kitchen window, chewing one of Indigo's wellies.

"W—what do you mean?" said Indigo, ignoring Graham as he stuck his head through the open window. Indigo had a billion questions. "Where have you come from? What is your name? How do you know they're missing?"

The bear-Creature sighed and sat back on her haunches.

"I am from the Unknown Wilderness. I am a Moonbear … My name is Callisto," said Callisto the Moonbear in a tuneful voice. Indigo and Quigley stared in amazement. Moonbears were about the rarest Creatures in all the Known and Unknown Worlds. There wasn't even a drawing in the *Abracadarium* because nobody had ever set eyes on one before.

"Moonbear's name is C–A–L–L–I–S–T–O," Indigo fingerspelled to Quigley. Quigley beamed and told Callisto his sign name, a pair of bat wings.

"Your parents were studying me in the wild," continued Callisto. "They were so excited to have found a Moonbear. My kind don't usually let humans too close … Moonbears are supposed to be able to hide themselves. Most can fly faster than a flash of lightning. Some of my kind have even been mistaken for shooting stars. But not me. I am different. I cannot fly. Ever since I was a cub, I have been afraid of heights and the thought of flying is …" The Moonbear gulped and looked ashamed. Indigo put a reassuring hand on Callisto's feathery wing. "Your parents found me on the mountainside, caught in a trap laid by hunters." The Moonbear held up a gigantic paw. "They were so kind to me. It took them a long time to nurse me back to health …

then, one morning … they were GONE."

Quigley's lip trembled. Queenie gave him a big squeeze. Even Olli and Umpf looked worried.

"But how did you know where to find us?" asked Indigo.

"Your parents had told me all about this house, about the Creatures who lived here. How they are all different, about how you" – Callisto snuffled her nose into each of their faces, covering Quigley's hair in slobber – "care for Creatures who need looking after. Your parents and I were all set to return here together … then they vanished. We must find them. Before it's too late."

"Hang on!" shouted Indigo, racing into the living room and returning with a postcard. "Mum and Dad sent us this. Maybe it could give us a clue to where they might've gone?"

Indigo read the postcard aloud.

Dear Indigo and Quigley,

We have made a truly INCREDIBLE discovery!
We are just bursting to show you our newest friend!
We want it to be a BIG surprise, so I won't say any
more now!

Our campsite is a bit lonely – we thought we
might see Bethesda Brolly or the Abernathys, but
they must still be out exploring. There aren't many
Creatures around, either. We looked everywhere for a
griffin we've been studying but he must've migrated.
Anyway, we'll be on our way home very soon indeed.
We just have one more stop to make – we've just
heard that a new ice cream parlour has opened (in
the Jungliest Jungle, of all places!). Apparently it's
run by two lovely folk who love magical Creatures,
just like us! We'll bring some ice cream home for you.

Lots of love,

Mum and Dad xxx

MONSTER MAIL

Indigo & Quigley Wilde
47 Jellybean Cresc.
Boggy Bottom
The Known World

"An ice cream parlour?" said Indigo. "Callisto, do you know where this is?"

Callisto shook her head.

"No … I lived in the mountains. And what is ice cream, anyway?"

"Right …" said Indigo, trying to make herself feel brave. "We need to leave right away. There's only one way I know of getting to the Unknown Wilderness …"

Quigley gulped.

"… WE NEED TO FIND A GLURK."

-THREE-
THE GLURK

A Glurk, if you don't already know, is a
magical doorway that lets you travel to the
Unknown World. They can appear anywhere,
at any time. When Indigo's great-great-
great-grandmother, Gertrude Wilde, was a
little girl, she had been having a lovely hot
bubble bath when a Glurk had opened in
the plughole and she was sucked into the
Unknown Wilderness, bubbles and all. She
had eventually magicked her way back,

but she had found the whole thing highly inconvenient, and, it was rumoured, never bathed again.

Indigo had been rescued by Philomena and Bertram Wilde as a baby from the Unknown Wilderness. She had been too little to remember her parents bringing her back to the Known World through a Glurk, but she did remember them returning a few years later with her brother, Quigley. That time, they had popped up in the garden pond.

"I just need to look at the *Abracadarium*," Indigo said, and she sprinted up to her bedroom to collect the old book from under her bed.

The *Abracadarium* was a Wilde heirloom. It contained all the useful (and sometimes not very useful) information about the Unknown World and its Creatures that had been documented by generations of Wildes. Indigo turned the crinkled, aged pages and found the section on inter-world travel.

Inter-World Travel

Glurks

Glurks, or "inter-world doorways" can be found anywhere in the Known and Unknown World. They are often in unlikely and unpredictable places. A Glurk never appears in the same place twice. The presence of a Glurk can be noted by the gathering of fairies. Fairies are drawn to the magic of the Glurk and will form a swarm around the doorway. Locating a swarm is the best-known way of identifying a Glurk. Other methods include running repeatedly into doors/trees/walls or other likely looking spots, and hoping for the best, OR ripping a hole in the World using magic. (We do not recommend this as it can lead to Big Trouble and Unlimited Chaos.)

Blue Glurk Fairy
(Caeruleum Glurkus Mediocris)

Most common. Found in urban and rural areas. Creates safe, stable Glurks.

Green Glurk Fairy
(Viridis Glurkus Mediocris)

Fairly common in forests and jungles. Creates reliable Glurks but they can be slow to travel through.

Rainbow Glurk Fairy
(Iridis Glurkus Mediocris)

Very rare. Found in highly magical areas. Rainbow Glurks are highly unstable and using one risks ripping a hole in a World. Use with caution.

Travelling by Glurk can be quite uncomfortable. Do not travel by Glurk if you've just had breakfast, or your toast may make a reappearance.

Gertie Wilde (27)

Indigo tried to think calmly. If they were going on an adventure, she should pack some useful things, just in case. Her parents had taught her: always be prepared. She carefully wedged the *Abracadarium* into her backpack along with her toothbrush and a torch. Then she took a battered old compass from her windowsill. It had belonged to her great-great-great-grandmother, and was the surest way of navigating around the Unknown World (the magic there sent normal compasses haywire). Indigo wrapped it safely in an old pair of bobbly socks before putting that in her bag, too.

Lastly, Indigo threw some food to the

newts on her bedside table and hurried back
downstairs.

"We need to look for fairies!" puffed Indigo
as she crashed back into the hallway. "Fairies
gather around Glurks."

"I've packed food!" signed Quigley, holding
up a bulging backpack.

Indigo turned to Queenie, Olli and Umpf.

"I don't know how long we will be,
but you are in charge. Don't forget to feed
Haystacks."

Queenie nodded grimly.

"Don't worry 'bout the house … we'll take
care of it. Just find your parents and … be safe,"
said Queenie in an oddly strained voice.

"UGGG!" said Olli and Umpf. Which Indigo
knew meant, "Don't worry, we will water
the plants."

"See you later, then," said Indigo, as she followed Quigley and Callisto out into the evening twilight. Turning back, she added weakly, "And Graham … do try not to eat everything while we are away, won't you?"

Graham burped loudly.

★

"Callisto, you can't be seen by Madam Grey," hissed Indigo as they walked out on to a deserted Jellybean Crescent. "She's bound to be out prowling."

Callisto moved noiselessly on her great black paws. "Climb on my back, it'll be faster," she whispered. "Although I can't fly ..." she added with an edge of shame in her voice. "I've always been too scared."

Indigo pulled Quigley on to Callisto's back just as Madam Grey sprang from behind a postbox, where she had been crouched with her gigantic binoculars. They stared at each other for a fraction of a second, then …

"RUN!" shouted Indigo.

JELLYBEAN CRES.

Callisto bounded forward as
Madam Grey shrieked after them.
The Moonbear was moving so fast, the
houses on either side blurred and Indigo
had to cling on for dear life. They thundered
down the street in a shower of stars and
Madam Grey was soon left far behind.

"That was close," panted Indigo, pushing
her hair out of her eyes as they made their
way into the park. The playground swings
hung silently in the moonlight. Indigo was
starting to feel anxious and a little bit hungry.

"What if we never get there? What if
we can't find a Glurk?" she signed to her
little brother. Quigley squeezed her hand
reassuringly.

Callisto stopped and gave a low hum, pointing a large paw in the direction of the playground. Right in the middle of the roundabout was a mist of tiny specks floating in the air. Indigo squinted through the darkness. If you hadn't been paying attention, you could easily have mistaken them for a cloud of midges.

"Yes!" she breathed. "Fairies! That's it! It's a Glurk!"

They bounded towards it.

"But how do we get IN?" signed Quigley.

"WE SPIN!" signed Indigo, a glint of excitement in her eyes. "Get on!"

The Moonbear clambered awkwardly on to the dilapidated old roundabout. Quigley held the rail. The fairies chattered and danced in the air above their heads as Indigo started to push. She pushed round and round, FASTER AND FASTER AND FASTER, and just as the ground felt like it was vanishing from beneath her feet, she jumped on. As the world began to go fuzzy at the edges, Indigo saw a horribly familiar shape hurtling towards them across the park.

It was Madam Grey and she was sprinting towards them, her dog Pebbles racing behind.

"NO!" shouted Indigo, as Madam Grey and Pebbles leapt straight at the roundabout. In a swirling SWOOSH of sound and colour, the Glurk pulled them all into the Unknown World with a POP.

-FOUR-

THE UNKNOWN WILDERNESS

They tumbled through nothingness and landed with a muffled crash amongst the soft leaves of a hairy acid-green plant. Indigo rubbed her head and groaned. As she helped Quigley to his feet and brushed gloop from Callisto's feathers, Indigo's eyes adjusted to the World they had fallen into. They were on the crest of a gigantic grassy hill.

Dotted amongst the waist-high
grass were the most extraordinary plants.
Some were toweringly tall and dripped
with syrupy ooze, while others were so
small Indigo had to get down on her hands
and knees to see them. Great jewel-winged
butterflies danced through the grass and the
whole place had the subtle flowery smell of
Parma violets.

"WOW!" said Indigo, staring around. There
were hills everywhere, poking upwards like
giant knobbly knees. In the distance, she
thought she could make out the shimmer
of the ocean. The air was hot and dry and
she felt like she was being
blown with a hairdryer.

Remembering Madam Grey, Indigo looked about in sudden panic. Their unfortunate neighbour had landed upside down in a bush. Only her legs were visible, bicycling the air frantically as she tried to free herself. Before Indigo could help, the bush gave an enormous SHUDDER, made a retching noise and spat Madam Grey out on to her bony bottom, Pebbles clutched in her trembling arms. The bush hiccupped, grumbled under its breath and became still.

"W—what ... what is this?" breathed Madam Grey, looking frantically around at the spectacular plants, the shimmering Moonbear and then at Indigo and Quigley, who were both trying to work out what on earth they were going to say.

"Errrm ..." started Indigo. But how do you explain that you've been sucked into

38

another world to somebody like Madam Grey? They were certain she couldn't blame THIS on an out-of-date lasagne.

"Well …" signed Quigley.

Callisto padded forward. Madam Grey looked like she was about to faint.

"This is the Unknown World …" said Callisto. "Well … this bit of it is called the Unknown Wilderness … and, more specifically, I think we are currently on one of the Oolith Hills." The Moonbear seemed to have decided that truth was the only option. Indigo gulped.

"Not many people in your world know about the Unknown World any more …" Callisto continued sadly. "It used to be that everyone knew about it … and you could get here much more easily … but nowadays, PEOPLE DON'T REALLY LIKE MAGIC."

Madam Grey stared at Callisto in horror, but it seemed the shock of finding herself in an entirely new world had left her speechless, as the only noise she could make was a high-pitched SQUEAK that sounded like a gerbil being sat on.

"What do we do with her?" signed Quigley, looking at his big sister in panic as the plant above them oozed a thick, syrupy blob of goo on to Madam Grey's head.

"We will have to just … bring her along," replied Indigo, who couldn't see any other option. She squinted towards the jungle. "Any guesses which way we should go?" she asked the Moonbear.

Callisto looked worried. "Ah … yes, well, you see the thing with the Oolith Hills is that they don't tend to … stay still."

"What do you mean they don't stay still?" asked Indigo faintly. But her question was answered before Callisto could say another word.

Their hill suddenly gave a huge LURCH and began to move. Madam Grey let out a strangled shriek. Indigo and Quigley held on tight to Callisto. The other hills were all moving, too, like a gigantic game of musical chairs. Their hill spun and shuddered, juddered and jiggled until Indigo thought she might be sick. Then, as quickly as it had started, the hill plonked itself down again with a great grating of rock and a sigh of settling earth.

Their view had completely changed. They had moved to the very edge of the range of hills and now, a vast jungle stretched out directly below them like a multicoloured sea.

"So, that's the Jungliest Jungle?" asked Indigo as she clambered to her feet.

Callisto nodded.

"But which way should we go?" Indigo asked, a little desperately. This world looked very BIG.

Quigley pointed excitedly into the trees.

Beyond the vast treetop ocean there was a thin trail of coloured smoke curling up into the sky.

"Crumping crumpets! Is that smoke? Good spot, Quig! Maybe it's Mum and Dad's campsite? Or the ice cream place?" Indigo pulled the battered compass from inside the pair of bobbly socks in her backpack.

The compass wasn't marked with north, south, east and west like a normal compass. This one had totally different markings that only made sense in the Unknown World: widdershins, sunwise, gubbins and yonder.

"The smoke is due sunwise. Unless anyone has a better idea, I think we should go that way," signed Indigo.

Feeling confident, she strode over the crest of the hill ...

... AND FELL RIGHT OFF THE EDGE.

– FIVE –

THE MARSH GNOMES

"AHHHHHH!" Indigo yelled as she plummeted downwards. Closing her eyes tight, she waited for the moment she hit the trees. But it never came. She opened her eyes and saw that she was floating on top of what looked like a cloud. She stretched out her hand and touched the fluffy pinkish surface. It was solid, like a yeti's woolly coat, but also somehow felt like it wasn't there.

"WAHOOOOO!"

47

Indigo looked up to see Quigley gleefully throwing himself off the ledge like a cannonball. He landed on the cloud and bounced back into the air as though he had hit a trampoline.

Indigo looked up at Callisto. The great bear was crouched on the edge of the hill as if she was about to take flight. Her eyes were scrunched up tight and she was trembling more than Madam Grey, who she held under a great paw like a sack of turnips.

"Don't worry, Callisto!" shouted Indigo. "The landing is soft!"

The bear shook her head and covered her eyes.

Just as Indigo was about to call out some more words of encouragement, a great plant snapped its toothy mouth at Pebbles. The little dog jumped high into the air and landed

on Callisto's head,
yowling. The bear
leapt in fright
and before she
knew it, she was
falling through the
air. Madam Grey's
mouth hung open in
a silent scream.

Callisto hit the cloud with a
soft WHUMP and slowly opened her eyes.

"I told you it was a soft landing!" laughed
Indigo in relief. "What is this stuff?" she
wondered aloud as she got shakily to her feet.
It was like standing on fuzzy jelly.

"It's mallowcloud," said Callisto, still
trembling.

"It's made by G-N-O-M-E-S," signed
Indigo, fingerspelling a bit because she

couldn't remember the sign for gnome.

"Gnomes?" signed Quigley, looking excited.

Madam Grey made the squashed gerbil noise again.

"Yes, gnomes," continued Callisto. "They make mallowcloud when they toast marshmallows, see."

She pointed a shaky claw at the ground below them.

The mallowcloud had sunk lower and was brushing the underside of the jungle trees.

The air was much cooler and wetter down in the shade of the umbrella-sized flowers and gigantic dripping leaves.

On the ground, in a little clearing between the patches of spiky plants and towering trunks, was a ring of giant spotty toadstools. Under the toadstools, there was a group of small Creatures dressed in multicoloured, mismatched clothes and gathered around a pink fire.

"Gnomes!" signed Quigley again, somersaulting with joy on his bouncy cloud.

Each gnome had a huge marshmallow speared on a stick and they were happily turning them in the flames as great puffs of bouncy mallowcloud billowed into the air.

"Oh, how lovely!" said Indigo as they jumped from the cloud to the soft ground below.

Callisto set Madam Grey down gently, but she crumpled face first into the leaves as if her knees weren't working.

When the mallowcloud touched the jungle floor, it popped with a little tinkling noise, just like the sound of a bell over the door of a sweet shop. Moments later, tiny pink and white blobs blossomed out of the soil.

"Marvellous!" cheeped a tinny voice. A small gnome wearing a pair of wellingtons hopped over and sprinkled something on the little blobs on the ground.

"What's that?" asked Indigo, puzzled.

"Sugar!" exclaimed the gnome. "Got to have sugar to grow …"

Indigo gasped. Where the tiny blobs had been, great squishy marshmallows had bloomed. The gnome plucked them from the ground and hurried back to the fire.

"Come, come!" he chirruped over his shoulder. "There's plenty for everyone!"

The other gnomes welcomed the travellers merrily. Indigo glanced at Madam Grey, who was being carried over Callisto's shoulder again. Her eyes were rather wild.

"Hello, dears," said a green-haired gnome wearing a fabulous set of dangly earrings. "So nice of you to join us Marsh Gnomes for our little party. Oh dear, what's wrong with your friend?"

"Oh … er … she's just in shock, I think," said Indigo as the gnome handed them little wooden plates piled high with hot sticky marshmallows.

The gnome looked at Madam Grey with concern. "Hmmm … Oh! Shhhh, the music is starting!"

In the middle of the clearing, a group of dazzlingly glittered gnomes had climbed on to one of the giant toadstools.

The largest and sparkliest cleared her throat and began to sing as the others strummed guitars, piped flutes and banged drums.

The sound was quite extraordinary. Callisto tapped her great paw along to the music and Quigley swayed to the vibrations of the drumbeat on the ground. Madam Grey had a glassy expression, as if she couldn't believe what her ears were hearing.

The sun was setting and the gnome party was in full swing. The effect of the sugary marshmallows and the offbeat melody made Indigo's head feel like TINY FIZZING BUBBLES were popping in her brain. She shook herself, trying to clear her thoughts, and suddenly remembered why they had come here. In all the drama, she had quite forgotten.

"Excuse me," Indigo said hazily to a gnome wearing a woolly poncho. He was humming tunelessly and completely out of rhythm with the music.

"Oh, hello," said the gnome airily.

"Can I just ask … well, we are here looking for our parents. They are Explorers, and they've gone missing. You might know them – Philomena and Bertram Wilde? We are looking for an ice cream parlour – it was the last place they …"

The music stopped. The gnomes stared at Indigo.

"We don't talk about …" spluttered the ponchoed gnome.

"And we suggest you don't talk about it, either," called the gnome singer. She looked suddenly quite fierce.

"Sorry," said Indigo, "but … we really need some help."

As the gnome opened her mouth to reply, there came a RUMBLING noise from deep in the jungle, and a tinkling tune that seemed totally out of place. Indigo looked at the other gnomes, but their instruments had all fallen to the ground. The tinkling tune grew louder, then faded slowly away on the breeze.

The gnomes all exchanged panicked glances.

"I said, we don't talk about it," said the singing gnome sharply. "I think you all ought to leave … NOW."

And with that, the plates were whipped from their hands and the gnomes marched them away from the warm fire and into the darkening jungle.

The dangly-earringed gnome hung back a little way from the group.

"Be careful, children," she whispered. "It's not just Explorers that have vanished … gnomes and all sorts of magical animals and plants have been disappearing. It's dangerous. Be careful!" And she squeezed Indigo's hand before running off after the other gnomes.

Indigo looked down – the gnome had pressed something small into her palm. It was a tube of Dr Gnasher's Extra Strength

Toothpaste (cuts through sugar like lightning!).

Confused, Indigo put it in her backpack and turned to her friends. The gloom of twilight had fallen on the jungle and the travellers were quite alone. Callisto wrapped her great warm wings around them for shelter, and her fur twinkled like starlight.

"Don't … don't worry, Pebbles. This is all just a b–b–bad dream, isn't it?" said Madam Grey in a tiny, strained voice. Pebbles whimpered.

"I'm afraid not," said Indigo.

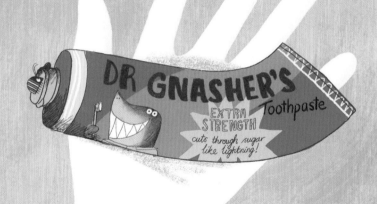

-SIX-

A NIGHT IN
THE JUNGLE

"First things first," said Indigo, trying not to let fear get the better of her, "let's have something to eat and drink. It must be way past dinner-time by now and those marshmallows have made me feel sick. Quig, what did you pack for us to …" But she trailed off as she began to unpack Quigley's bulging backpack.

"Marmalade? Quigley … did you only pack marmalade?" Indigo signed,

turfing jar after jar from the voluminous bag. Quigley nodded, looking sheepish.

"We were in a rush!" he signed. Indigo's tummy growled.

"Is the news on yet, Pebbles?" asked Madam Grey in a dazed voice. "Is it time for an omelette?" Her eyes were pointing in opposite directions. "As long as it's not lasagne again … I was on the toilet for weeks …"

Quigley GIGGLED.

"OK," Indigo signed, rubbing her head. "OK. We just need to think … there must be something else to eat around here somewhere. Mum and Dad always said the Jungliest Jungle was jam-packed with delicious fruit."

"I wouldn't go poking around in the bushes too much, if I were you …" signed Callisto, as Quigley rummaged in the leaves of a huge plant.

"Just looking for—" Quigley signed, but stopped quickly when the leaves began to quiver. The low rumbling noise filled the trees again and the distant sound of a weird tinkly music wafted through the jungle. A cloud of birds took to the air as the branches shook.

"Climb on my back!" Callisto whispered urgently, and Indigo jumped up first, signing to Quigley to follow. But before he could, a huge dark shape came crashing into their clearing, followed by another, and another, and another …

"STAMPEDE!" yelled Indigo. "RUN!" And in total chaos, they turned and fled through the trees. Indigo managed to grab Quigley and haul him on to Callisto's back. The Creatures were stampeding at full force and it was all they could do to run alongside them so they didn't get trampled.

"Callisto, I know you can't fly but you've got to keep running, OK?" shouted Indigo.

Callisto scrunched her eyes tight again and nodded, her paws beating against the earth faster and faster. Indigo knew the Moonbear was worrying that she couldn't run fast enough.

"Up there!" Indigo cried, pointing at a large branch that had grown down to the jungle floor. Callisto leapt for it and they bounded up and away from the ferocious clawed feet of the stampede. Indigo pulled them higher into the massive tree, out of the way of the panicked Creatures below. Callisto was trembling.

"I'm sorry!" she cried, covering her face with her paws. "If I could just be braver …"

Indigo squeezed her paw gently. "You ARE brave. We could never have outrun that

64

without you. Can you see Madam Grey? Or Pebbles? They were still in shock – did they even run?" She tried desperately to see anything through the gloom and the chaos of the running Creatures.

At first glance the Creatures looked like giant, hairy ostriches, running upright on two scaly, clawed legs, but as flock after flock stampeded past, Indigo saw they had huge feathery tails and big banana-shaped beaks with a great bony horn that curved up and over their small heads. They would have looked quite funny if they hadn't just nearly trampled them into HUMAN JAM.

"What are they?" signed Quigley, pointing down at the feathery Creatures.

Indigo rooted around in her backpack and pulled out the *Abracadarium*. She turned to the section on Jungle-dwelling Creatures.

"They're rhinostriches," Indigo said. "It says they're harmless …" she scoffed. "Yes, unless they squash you to death."

They were quiet for a while. Indigo scribbled in the *Abracadarium* to update the entry on rhinostriches and Quigley sat in Callisto's great paws, eating marmalade and watching the endless stampede below for any sign of Madam Grey and Pebbles.

"I wonder what made the rhinostriches so scared …" signed Indigo.

★

Night had fallen and it had started to rain by the time the stampede had passed. The jungle HUMMED and BUZZED and there was still no sign of Madam Grey or Pebbles. Indigo felt unbearably guilty.

"If I'd just shaken her off properly at the Glurk, she'd never have come with us," she said sadly.

Quigley made a heart shape with their hands and Indigo felt a little bit better. They slid out of the tree and Indigo checked the compass.

"Right, I think that smoke we saw was this way ..."

RHINOSTRICH
ᐱᖏᐃᗐᖴᎦᐟᐤᐱᖏᏟᎦ

Flock of rhinostriches nearly squished us into jam! Indigo

Distribution: Jungliest Jungle
Unknown Wilderness
(Extinct in Known World)

Diet: Gooba berries

Harmless but unpredictable
(flightless)

3m

3 talons on each foot ↓

Egg incubation: 42 days

50cm

tracks

male mating plumage
Females have shorter tails.

chicks

They traipsed through the wet jungle as the darkness deepened. They clambered over logs, scaled rocks and crossed streams but the jungle just got denser and emptier.

The rain was so heavy it felt like standing under a running tap and there wasn't a single bit of Indigo that wasn't soaked. Just as she thought she couldn't possibly get any wetter, her foot slipped and she sank waist-deep into an oozing, stinking bog.

Indigo sighed.

Callisto and Quigley both sank with a great SQUELCH behind her, just as the weird tinkling music drifted softly towards them on the breeze again. Indigo froze. In the distance,

she could make out two bright
lights slowly pootling through the
soggy trees.

"Is it a car?" asked Indigo, as the
rumbling grew louder and the lights swept
through the jungle, throwing them into
shadow.

They struggled to free themselves, trying
desperately to get a better look, but by the
time Indigo had struggled out of the thick,
clinging ooze and pulled Quigley and Callisto
to safety, the tinkling music was long gone.

"What do you think it was?" signed Quigley, looking at Callisto.

"I don't know … it did look a bit like a car, but it made some weird tinkly music, and there are no roads in the Jungliest Jungle," Callisto replied.

"Maybe someone lives near here?" signed Quigley.

"Are there any houses here, though?" said Indigo, pulling off her backpack and rummaging inside for the *Abracadarium*.

She looked closely at the map. "No," she sighed. "There aren't. There's a lake and … about a billion trees. That smoke was near the foot of the mountains, though, so if we keep going sunwise we should eventually find … SOMETHING."

-SEVEN-

KNICKERBOD'S ICE CREAM

The inky black of night slowly melted into dawn and as the sun rose, the leaves and flowers were tinged with soft pink and gold. The rain had stopped and Indigo's wet, slimy clothes began to steam in the sunlight. She kept checking the compass and straining her ears for any sound of Madam Grey, Pebbles or the weird tinkly music.

"I thought there would be more Creatures around," Indigo observed as they walked.

"Mum and Dad always talk about how they can't go two steps here without bumping into some sort of amazing Creature. They said this place was overflowing with magical stuff, but it's very … QUIET?"

"Hmmmm," said Callisto. "Well, it's like that Marsh Gnome said, lots of Creatures have been disappearing … maybe there aren't any left? Maybe the ones that are left are hiding?"

Worry made Indigo's tummy feel even more hollow. She was sure the disappearance of her parents and the Creatures must be linked in some way.

As they walked, a strange smell floated towards them through the trees.

"Can you smell that?" asked Indigo groggily.

Quigley nodded and signed, "It smells like peanut butter and cookie dough and marmalade!"

Indigo frowned. "No, it doesn't! It smells like doughnuts and roast potatoes and … apple sauce!"

Callisto sniffed the air and growled. "It's very strange. I've never smelled anything like it before. It smells … like MAGIC."

As they rounded a bend on the narrow path they'd been following, they saw a great pool of watery dawn sunlight streaming through the trees. The strange smell grew stronger. Indigo felt like it was reeling her in like a fish on a line. Quigley licked his lips.

"I think it's a clearing!" said Indigo excitedly, as she ran to the edge of the trees.

Her mouth fell open in astonishment.

In the middle of the clearing was a huge building, painted in shocking pink. It had seven floors and was so crooked that it was a wonder it was still standing. Flowerpots

overflowing with what looked like candyfloss
sat on every windowsill and the ground
floor had huge windows displaying the most
fantastical array of ICE CREAMS.

"Crumping crumpets … I think we've
found the ice cream parlour," signed Indigo in
wonder.

Quigley squealed with delight and pointed up at the roof. It was made of hundreds of biscuit tiles, complete with thick toffee sauce and finished with thousands of sprinkles. Humongous chimneys made from wafers poked out of it, puffing out the magic-scented smoke. The overall effect was quite overwhelming.

"I ... I think that's the smoke you saw from the hills, Quig," breathed Indigo in amazement. The smell was overpowering now they stood so close. Every time Indigo breathed in she could taste the flavours in the air.

Despite its crookedness, the building wasn't run down. In fact, the paint seemed fresh and what looked like a brand-new sign had been nailed above the shop windows.

Indigo read:

"Knickerbod's Ice Cream Parlour … Our ice cream is MAGIC."

Beneath this sign hung a smaller board.

"For a Truly Magical Experience, why not stay in one of our luxury cabins? Eight-course ice cream breakfast included."

"Reckon there's anyone to ask for help?" signed Quigley, eyeing the ice cream display hungrily.

"I guess we'd better take a look," signed Indigo.

Before Indigo could raise her hand to knock, the shop door opened and a woman stepped out. At first, Indigo thought her eyes were playing tricks on her. The woman was tall and fair, with pink hair that was whipped into a twirl on top of her head. She wore a pastel-coloured shawl and a pink tea dress, over-large pink glasses and powder-blue boots. She was twirling a candy-coloured umbrella in her delicate hands. Indigo thought that she looked like a human ice cream. She wouldn't have been surprised if the woman had just melted all over the floor right in front of them.

Indigo was about to say hello when a man appeared at the woman's side. Indigo knew who he was at once, as his face was the same as in the picture painted on the sign above their heads.

He wore a white chef's apron and a funny little hat that was perched atop a spectacular blue quiff. He had a twirly whirl of a moustache that looked like curled liquorice, and a radiant smile.

"Why, hello, young Explorers!" he exclaimed jauntily. "I am Mr Knickerbod and this" – he gestured at the pink-haired woman

– "is Ms Darling. Welcome, welcome, to our new little enterprise! Knickerbod's Ice Cream Parlour ..." He beamed and added, "and LUXURY FIVE-STAR GUEST CABINS!" He puffed out his chest proudly and twirled his hand at the violently pink building.

Indigo shook herself and cleared her throat, signing as she spoke.

"H–hello," she said. "I'm Indigo, this is my brother, Quigley, and this is our friend, Callisto. We are looking for ... well ... a few people actually. Have you seen a woman with a little brown dog?"

Mr Knickerbod and Ms Darling exchanged troubled glances.

"No, no ... We haven't seen anybody at all ... And a dog, you say? No, no dogs," Mr Knickerbod said, sounding concerned.

"Have you seen our parents, then?

Philomena and Bertram Wilde? They're EXPLORERS and they've gone missing … they said they were coming here, look …" Indigo showed them the postcard. "Have you seen them? Could you take us to their campsite?"

"Oh, my dears," said Ms Darling, and she breezed towards them. She glanced at Callisto with interest, then spoke to Indigo. "You poor wee chicks. First things first. I bet you're hungry? Clarence, they're soaked right through," she said, turning to Mr Knickerbod.

"Well, we can't have that," Mr Knickerbod said bracingly. "I'm sure we can find a cabin for you, and I think it's ice cream all round."

Ms Darling led them through the door of the parlour. Indigo gazed at the stupendous displays of ice cream inside.

There was stack upon stack of different-coloured scoops of ice cream, kept cold by clouds of freezing, glittering fog. Towers of cones lined one wall – some dipped in toffee or chocolate, some shaped like animals and some that spiralled like unicorn horns. There were trays of nougat, sprinkles, chocolate chips and sweets, and shiny silver spoons and scoops hanging neatly on hooks. At the back of the parlour, they walked through a large stock-room where more boxes were piled in neat stacks. Indigo saw one with the stamp MARSH GNOME MALLOWS and another labelled SPOTTY GOZZPICKLER DUST.

They left the stock-room by a small back
door and emerged again into the sunlight. All
the while, Knickerbod waffled on proudly
about his ice cream.

"You just wait until you've tried it. It is
the very best there is. We've had to expand
operations recently – we now ship to the
whole of the Known and Unknown World

Top-quality production and top-quality ingredients. We built this parlour about six months ago … of course with all the ice-cream-making equipment, there isn't really room for guests inside the main building, but we wanted to give our guests the full Knickerbod experience … so we've built these instead …" He twirled his hands elaborately, like a mayor presenting a new statue, and Indigo saw what he was talking about.

Behind the parlour sat a dozen little cabins, painted in cheerful pastel colours. Each had a shiny brass number nailed to its door and the same candyfloss flowerpots on each windowsill. Indigo, however, was distracted from the cabins by the gigantic ice-skating rink that lay between them. Ice-skating was one of Indigo's favourite things to do ever.

Mr Knickerbod handed Indigo a little brass key with the number 7 dangling from it. He showed them into the pastel-blue cabin with a flourish.

"I hope you'll find this comfortable. If there's anything you need, do not hesitate to ask. Ms Darling, will you bring our young Explorers some ice cream?"

Ms Darling smiled and nodded.

"You wee chicks get yourselves comfy and I'll pop back in a moment with something for you, OK?"

"T–thank you," stammered Indigo. "But do you think you might also be able to ... well, to help us look for our parents? We could use all the help we can get."

"Of course, of course!" boomed Mr Knickerbod, twirling his moustache. "But first ... EAT!"

A pink fire glittered merrily in the cabin fireplace as Indigo and Quigley dried themselves off. Callisto shook her wings and stretched out in front of the hearth.

Ms Darling appeared soon after, with a tray stacked high with dishes, bowls and glasses.

"Here we are," she said gently as she sat the tray down on the table between them. Indigo had never seen such ice cream. Towers of butterscotch dripping in toffee sauce, strawberry ripple with caramel banana. Wafers shaped like dragonflies that flapped their wings, sprinkles that glowed like miniature stars, and tiny marzipan unicorns that galloped through the sauce and left little trails of rainbow-coloured glitter. It really was MAGICAL! Indigo tried it all (except the

chocolate – she thought chocolate tasted like socks and mud) and it was all deliciously tasty. Quigley was in a world of his own – he had spent the last five minutes face-down in a sundae dish.

"Are these Marsh Gnome marshmallows?" Indigo asked Ms Darling, watching Quigley shovelling the mallows into his mouth.

Ms Darling looked a little taken aback, but smiled and said, "Yes, dear, they are. How do you know about the Marsh Gnomes?"

"We met them when we first arrived … I sort of fell off a hill, straight into their camp." Indigo laughed. The sugar was making her feel GIDDY.

"Oh … well, yes, we do a little trade with the Marsh Gnomes. Have you tried the bubblegum?"

Indigo thought vaguely that Ms Darling was trying to change the subject, but her sugar-filled, exhausted brain couldn't think straight.

"You will help us look for our parents, and Madam Grey?" she asked, rubbing her eyes.

Ms Darling smiled.

"Of course, but I think you all need to sleep first. I'll pop by later and we can make a plan."

-EIGHT-
THE HUNT FOR CLUES

Indigo curled up on one of the squashy beds. She desperately wanted to start searching for their parents and Madam Grey, but it had been a wild night and her brain felt like it had been trampled by rhinostriches.

Before she knew it, she was being gently shaken awake by Quigley.

"Mr Knickerbod and Ms Darling are here. They want to help us look for Mum and Dad!" he signed excitedly.

"Ready for the search?" boomed Mr Knickerbod. He was still wearing his pristine chef's apron, but had pulled on a pair of camouflage trousers and had replaced his chef's hat with a large pith helmet that looked familiar to Indigo.

Ms Darling had swapped her umbrella for an elaborately carved walking cane.

"Did you sleep well?" she asked kindly, as she helped Mr Knickerbod haul a large rucksack on to his back.

"Yes ... Hey, wait!" Indigo gasped in disbelief. "That rucksack ... that's Dad's camping rucksack!" She remembered all the times she'd seen her father unpack and repack it. Quigley bounded over and nodded frantically, pointing at the bag. Callisto sniffed it and gave a low growl.

"Oh, this old thing?" said Mr Knickerbod in surprise. "I got it from our lost property

box … I think we found it in the jungle, didn't
we, Elspeth?" he said, turning to Ms Darling.

"Oh yes, that's right. We found it … and
that hat," she said airily.

"Yes! That's Mum's hat!" Indigo cried.
"Can you show us where you found them?"

"Of course, of course, young Explorers!" said Mr Knickerbod, pulling a map from his jacket pocket. "Follow me, I have a carefully planned route … We don't want to stray off the path, there are all sorts of dangerous Creatures in these parts. Yetis, trolls … very dangerous indeed."

Indigo frowned – the only yetis and trolls she knew weren't dangerous in the slightest.

But there were no Creatures to be seen at all. The jungle was silent and hot. Quigley sat on Callisto's back as they plodded slowly through the undergrowth. Occasionally, Mr Knickerbod would stop and look behind a rock or under a bush with a flourish. Then, he'd loudly exclaim, "ONWARDS! ONWARDS! They can't just have … disappeared. We'll find them soon, I'm sure of it." And they'd set off again.

By lunchtime they had made it to their parents' campsite. It turned out to be a small clearing in the trees, with a few charred logs in a fire pit in the centre.

Callisto sniffed the ground, Quigley riding high on her back. "This is their campsite, all right," she hummed. "I last saw them here … I went into the mountains to find food. I was gone for two days, but when I returned, they'd gone. I didn't know they were planning to go to the parlour …"

"Well, they never turned up at the parlour, did they, Clarence?" said Ms Darling.

"No. And we've thoroughly explored this campsite. I doubt there will be any other clues here," Mr Knickerbod said confidently.

Just then, Quigley tugged urgently on Callisto's fur and pointed up at one of the trees.

"What is it, Quig?" asked Indigo.

Quigley steered the Moonbear over to the tree, stood up on her back and reached his hand into a crack in the trunk. He pulled out a tatty piece of mud-streaked paper. There were drawings of plants and animals on one side and on the back there was a note in unfamiliar handwriting:

Dear Philomena and Bertram,

I've been conducting research in the area and am alarmed to report that Creatures seem to be disappearing. I am setting off now to see if I can get to the bottom of it. I couldn't get in touch with the Abernathys or Professor Atakuma. I've not seen them for days and I don't know where they have gone either. If you see them, tell them that something very grave is happening in the Jungle. We must find out where the Creatures have gone.

See you soon,

Bethesda Brolly, Explorer

MISSING!
Eric the unicorn
griffin
marsh gnomes x10
fairies
Caspar dragon
Spotty Gozzpickler

"Who's Bethesda Brolly?" Quigley signed.

"She's another Explorer," said Callisto. "I don't think your parents ever got this note. It must've blown into that tree. They never said anything to me."

"The Marsh Gnomes were right, then. Magical Creatures are going missing! It sounds to me like Bethesda, the Abernathys and the professor are missing, too?" Indigo turned and put a worried hand on Callisto's thick fur. "Goodness, this is bigger than we thought."

"Well, what a to-do," Mr Knickerbod said briskly. "No doubt the poor souls were eaten by goblins. This place is alive with them."

Ms Darling wrinkled her nose in disgust.

"Hmm … well, not all goblins are bad," said Indigo, frowning. She thought of Queenie back at Jellybean Crescent, with a pang of homesickness.

"I wouldn't be at all surprised if some Creature was behind all of these disappearances. The Jungliest Jungle is a very dangerous place indeed," Ms Darling said.

Indigo folded the paper neatly into the *Abracadarium*. As she put the book into her backpack, her hand brushed the tube of Dr Gnasher's toothpaste. She took it out and stared blankly at it. Something wasn't right. She thought of her parents, her wonderful home and the Creatures – her friends – who lived there. It filled her with renewed determination. She pocketed the toothpaste and stood up.

"Come on," she said. "WE'VE GOT TO KEEP LOOKING."

After hours of searching under every bush, climbing into every hollow tree and clambering over every rock, they hadn't found any more clues. Indigo still felt guilty about Madam Grey and got a sad pang in her tummy when she thought about it.

That evening, Indigo, Quigley and Callisto sat around the crackling fire in their cabin, looking at the map and discussing where they should search next.

"We could go up into the mountains?" suggested Indigo. Callisto nodded.

"I think we ought to sleep. We will need all our energy tomorrow. The Mogote Mountains aren't for the faint-hearted," she said grimly.

Indigo wasn't sure how long she'd been asleep when she JERKED suddenly awake. There was the unmistakable sound of a dog barking outside. Indigo thought immediately of Pebbles, Madam Grey's little dog, and leapt out of bed. She shook Quigley and he sat up slowly, rubbing his eyes. Next to him, where Callisto had been sleeping, there was just an empty, crumpled blanket.

"Quigley," Indigo signed in the half-darkness. "WHERE IS CALLISTO?"

—NINE—
THE NIGHT RUN

Indigo put her shoes on as fast as she could and pulled a bewildered Quigley out into the night.

"Callisto?" Indigo called softly. The dog barked again.

"Quig, I think Pebbles is out here somewhere … I can hear him!" Indigo signed. "But where is Callisto?" she added.

A bright light shone suddenly through the darkness and they hurried to hide behind one of the other cabins. Out on the driveway, a vast van sat with its engine running and lights blazing. Quigley tugged Indigo's sleeve.

"It's an ice cream van!" he signed.

It was the most extraordinary ice cream van Indigo had ever seen. It had massive monster-truck wheels that were so huge, Indigo could've stood inside them, and the paintwork was eye-wateringly pink, even in the darkness. Indigo could just make out the words "Knickerbod's Ices" on the side of the van and, underneath, the line OUR ICE CREAM IS MAGIC!

It had a huge loudspeaker on the roof playing a pleasant tinkling tune that reminded Indigo of hot summer days at the seaside … and also of stampeding rhinostriches, angry gnomes and stinking bogs.

"That music … I heard—" began Indigo,

but just then, the unmistakable figures of
Mr Knickerbod and Ms Darling appeared,
carrying a huge box between them.

Indigo heard Ms Darling's hushed voice.
"Turn the music off, Clarence! Turn it off!
You'll wake them up!"
The music stopped.

They heaved the box into the back of the
van, hopped in and began to drive slowly away.

"Quick, let's follow!" said Indigo.

"We'll never keep up!" signed Quigley.

"We've GOT to try!" Indigo said as she
pulled her little brother out into the darkness.
They ran for far longer than either of them

knew they were able to run for, over mossy logs and through thick mud. Eventually, they panted to a stop as the ice cream van pulled up sharply next to an ominous wall of rock.

"We're at the foot of the Mogote Mountains!" Indigo signed, peering out from behind a thick tree trunk.

They watched as Mr Knickerbod and Ms Darling appeared from the back of the van, hauling the huge box. They struggled and groaned as they heaved it towards the rockface.

"Where are they going?" Indigo whispered, but Quigley pointed and gasped.

Mr Knickerbod had taken a large, long-handled ice cream spoon from his pocket and slotted it into a roughly cut hole in the rock. With a CRACK, the spoon turned and a doorway, cut straight into the rock face, slid open. They hoisted the box through the doorway and vanished from sight.

"QUICK! Before it closes!" signed Indigo frantically, and, without thinking it through at all, she pulled Quigley from behind their tree and through the closing doorway.

-TEN-

THE SECRET PARLOUR

Behind the door was a tightly spiralling stone staircase that vanished downwards into gloom. Indigo could hear shuffling footsteps and Mr Knickerbod complaining about the heaviness of the box.

Indigo and Quigley crept quietly down the steps. There was nowhere else to go. If Mr Knickerbod or Ms Darling came back up the steps now, they were done for. They were both dizzy by the time they reached a stone

hallway at the bottom of the stairs. The walls
were lined with portraits – all dressed in the
same chef's uniform that Mr Knickerbod
wore. Some of them looked very old. Quigley
squeezed Indigo's hand and they sneaked
down the hallway to another open door

Indigo peered cautiously through and had to clap her hands to her mouth to stop herself from screaming.

Beyond the door was a vast chamber of roughly cut rock. Indigo looked around in complete dismay. Along every edge of the cavern there were Creatures, and each and every one seemed to be TRAPPED – stuck in place by some sort of thick, solid gloop.

Indigo had quite forgotten that she and Quigley were supposed to be staying out of sight.

Along the wall closest to her there were bottles of fairies, glowing dully in the darkness, and a line of trolls whose eyes grew round when they saw her. A beautiful unicorn was stuck to the floor. The magical glow from his horn had nearly gone out.

Indigo didn't want to look further, but she had to. Pulling Quigley after her, she tiptoed into the cavern. Everywhere they looked, there were more Creatures. Indigo recognised a great snortlephant, a griffin, and in the far corner, a huge dragon, all stuck fast inside the horrible goo.

There were machines, too, all whirring arms and flashing lights. In a dark corner,

a group of Marsh Gnomes in a glass tank sat around a small fire. They were miserably toasting marshmallows, but the billowing mallowcloud was being sucked away through a huge pipe. Every now and then, marshmallows would pop out of the other end of the pipe into great glass jars marked KNICKERBOD'S MALLOWS! OUR MALLOWS ARE MAGIC! There were shelves lined with boxes of ingredients, too, all labelled with Mr Knickerbod's smiling face: trays of strawberry laces and sparkling gumdrops, glowing vials of unicorn sprinkles and hundreds of bottles of toffee sauce. And there was the smell again. That funny smell that had lured them to the ice cream parlour. The smell of magic.

Anger rose in Indigo like she had never known. She turned to Quigley, but too late. Mr Knickerbod had appeared from the gloom, throwing long ropes of strawberry lace around each of them and reeling them in like a pair of sardines.

"Why, it's our little Explorers!" he said, all trace of his usual jolly manner gone. "Too nosy for your own good! You're going to meet the same sticky end as your parents." He marched them over to the far side of the cavern, past hundreds of trapped Creatures, who all looked desperately out at them.

Mr Knickerbod pushed a button and a huge vat of toffee sauce began slowly churning.

"A quick dunk should do it." Mr Knickerbod laughed, hauling Indigo and Quigley up the steps to the lip of the

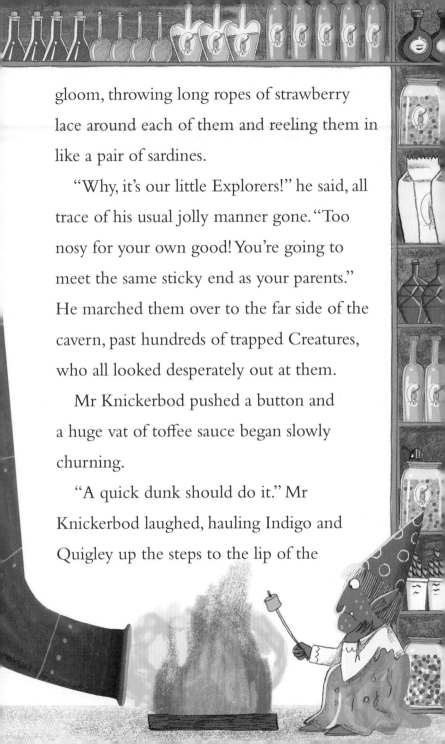

enormous churning drum.

Indigo teetered on the edge, then Mr Knickerbod gave her a sharp SHOVE into the warm sticky sauce. Quigley plopped in behind her. She tried to grab him as they both sank up to their knees, then their armpits …

Just as Indigo could see Quigley's chin about to go under, Mr Knickerbod hauled them out again, cackling. The sauce began to harden, until Indigo and Quigley could barely move a muscle.

But the anger hadn't gone from Indigo yet.

"You've been STEALING magical

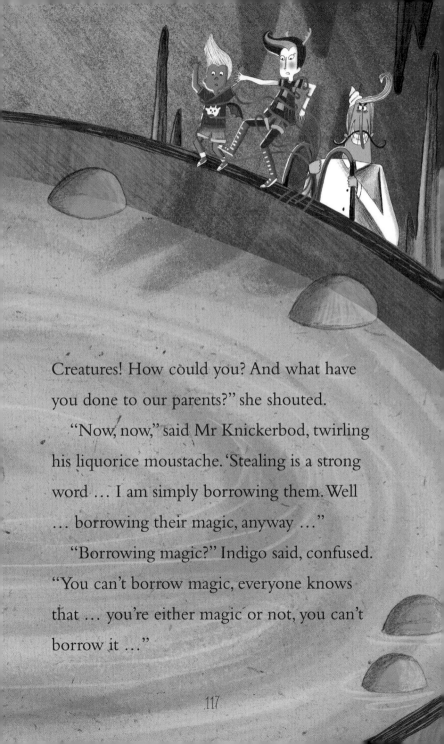

Creatures! How could you? And what have you done to our parents?" she shouted.

"Now, now," said Mr Knickerbod, twirling his liquorice moustache. 'Stealing is a strong word ... I am simply borrowing them. Well ... borrowing their magic, anyway ..."

"Borrowing magic?" Indigo said, confused. "You can't borrow magic, everyone knows that ... you're either magic or not, you can't borrow it ..."

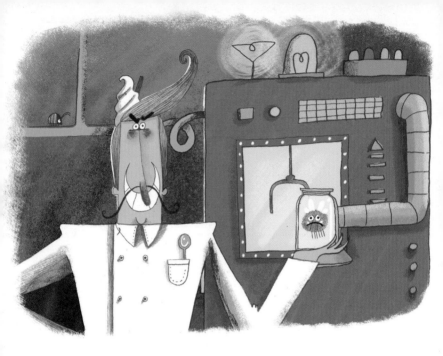

"Oh, but you CAN. See …" And Mr
Knickerbod flicked a switch. The cavern was
flooded with light. The magical Creatures all
began to shift uncomfortably.

"Take this fairy, for example … not that
magical, but, still … it has some magic." He
put a little fairy inside a jar and attached the
jar to one of the machines. There were tubes
and buttons and a control pad with all sorts of
funny knobs and dials. It reminded Indigo of

an ice cream maker. She gulped.

"I simply attach this bottle … and press these buttons … and ta-dah!" The machine WHIRRED into life. The fairy glowed momentarily brighter than it should, then the light was sucked away, just like the gnome's mallowcloud, down the tube and into the bottle. Mr Knickerbod took the bottle and corked it.

"There … freshly bottled magic. Now I can mix it into my ice cream and create the most magnificent creations in the whole of the Known and Unknown World. Think of the money, think of the fame! I will be the most famous ice cream maker since my great-great-great-great-great- … er … great-grandfather, Sir Balthazar Sprinkle!"

But Indigo wasn't listening. She was looking at the fairy. Where it had once glowed softly blue, its light had now completely gone out. Indigo felt tears prick her eyes.

"How could you?" she hissed. "I ate that ice cream and … and … How could you?"

"Easy peasy, it's all about the power." Knickerbod laughed again. "Ah, hello, Elspeth."

Ms Darling appeared at the doorway, wheeling poor, beautiful Callisto in a glass box.

"No!" Indigo cried.

"Be quiet, silly girl!" snarled Mr Knickerbod. He tied their strawberry-lace ropes to two hooks and pulled a lever that sent Indigo and Quigley lurching up into the gloom of the ceiling.

Indigo tried to kick her legs but they were held tight by the toffee sauce.

"GAHHHH!" she shouted in frustration.

"Indigo …? Quigley …? Is that you?" came a familiar voice out of the gloom.

Indigo's heart jumped as she tried to spin round, staring into the darkness.

"MUM? D—DAD?"

- ELEVEN -
TRAPPED

"Indigo! Quigley! Oh, no, we didn't want you captured … Oh, no, no, no!" cried Philomena. It appeared that she, too, had been wrapped in strawberry laces and dunked in the hard-setting sauce. Now that Indigo's eyes were adjusting to the darkness, she could make out several other people suspended from the ceiling beside her.

"Get a grip, Philomena," said a sharp female voice to Indigo's right. "We need to

think. If that man gets his hands on that bear's magic … well …"

"Yes, we need to think of a way … there must be a way …" hissed a man's voice behind them.

"But what, Bernhardt? We've tried everything," replied another voice.

"Who … who are you all?" Indigo asked.

"Ah, yes … I'm Bernhardt Abernathy and this is my wife, the Enchantress Cleopatra."

"And I," said the sharp voice, "am Professor Gazania Atakuma … botanist."

"Um … hello," came a fourth voice. "I'm Bethesda Brolly. I've not long been here … came in just before your parents, as a matter of fact."

"Knickerbod and Darling captured us all, my love," said the familiar voice of Indigo's father. "We saw a coupon in the newspaper — you know how I do love a coupon — 10% off at their ice cream parlour …"

"Do get on with it, dear," said Philomena.

"Ah yes … well, we turned up expecting a double scoop of chocolate ice cream with a dash of strawberry sauce … the next thing we know we woke up here dangling upside down and covered in goo. We had wondered where the others had gone. Turned out, they were here, too! They couldn't risk us ruining their plans, I suppose," he said sadly.

"And none of you can get out?" asked Indigo.

"No, my love," said Philomena wistfully.

"I do fear we may just about be done for."

Indigo was desperate. She could hear the clanks of the tubes being connected to Callisto's box. The Moonbear was frantic. There must be something – anything – they could do. They couldn't let Mr Knickerbod take Callisto's magic.

"We will need an extra-large jar to collect it all!" said Mr Knickerbod gleefully.

Indigo wiggled her hand under the toffee sauce. It hadn't fully set yet and there was a little bit of give in the thick ooze. She inched her hand into her pocket and felt the smooth tube of toothpaste she had put there at the campsite. Little by little, she wiggled it out. The sauce was setting harder now, and it was getting more and more difficult to move her hand. But with one last GIGANTIC PUSH, her hand burst through the sauce and was free.

Indigo reached out and squeezed Quigley's shoulder to let him know she had a plan. There was no time for her to explain, but Quigley nodded and smiled bravely.

Indigo could hear Mr Knickerbod laughing as he sorted through his jars. She unscrewed the toothpaste cap. When it was off, she squeezed the paste out on to the thick toffee. When the toothpaste hit the toffee sauce, it began to FIZZ and SWELL and FOAM like a bottle of fizzy drink that had been shaken up.

The other prisoners watched her with interest and confusion.

Indigo squeezed blob after blob of toothpaste on to the toffee sauce. It was working! The toothpaste was doing exactly what it said on the tube – cutting through sugar like lightning. Slowly, Indigo felt her arms and legs loosen and then …

"What's going on up there?" bellowed Mr
Knickerbod.

But it was too late. Indigo was free. She
dropped from the ceiling into a giant pile of
mallows. Mr Knickerbod advanced on her
like a grizzly bear but before he could reach
her, there was a CRASH and the door to the
chamber flew open.

Indigo's jaw hit the floor of the cave.

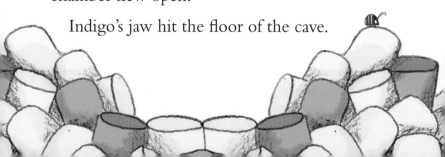

—TWELVE—
UNEXPECTED HELP

"M–Madam Grey?" Indigo whispered, so amazed she had to sink back into the marshmallows.

It definitely looked like Madam Grey, but it was also nothing like the Madam Grey that Indigo and Quigley knew so well. Gone were her boring grey clothes and neatly parted hair, replaced by a weird smock made of brightly coloured feathers and what looked like a crown made of leaves and twigs. Her hair was wild, she was covered in dirt and grime and she was riding – actually RIDING – a rhinostrich, like a warrior going into battle. A huge herd of rhinostriches flapped and squawked and pecked behind her and Pebbles was tucked under her arm, looking dazed.

"Who on earth are you?" Mr Knickerbod shrieked.

"I am Madam Edwina Grey, and I am here for Indigo and Quigley," yelled Madam Grey, looking positively fierce.

Indigo couldn't
believe it. Madam Grey had
come to rescue them, and
what was more … she seemed
to be quite enjoying herself!

Mr Knickerbod laughed coldly.
"Too late, you ridiculous woman, I'm just
about to—"

With a YODELLING SCREECH, Madam
Grey and the rhinostrich herd charged into the
chamber, sweeping Mr Knickerbod off his feet.

Ms Darling was knocked sideways by a
flapping rhinostrich. Indigo ran to Callisto's
box. She pulled out the wrinkled tube of
toothpaste and squeezed until a tiny drop
splattered out on to the glass. It fizzed and
foamed until a small hole appeared in the glass.

"What do they put in this stuff?" Indigo
breathed, and she watched in awe as the

Moonbear crouched, scrunching her eyes
tight shut, then exploded from the box in a
shower of light and stardust.

"Callisto!" cried Indigo, leaping towards
the Moonbear.

"Are you OK?" she gasped. The Moonbear
nodded fiercely, her fur sparkling with a
thousand stars.

"Listen," Indigo said, staring into the bear's great face. "I know you're afraid of heights, but do you think you can try to fly? We need to get the others down … we need to stop this!" she said, gesturing at the imprisoned Creatures.

Callisto scrunched her eyes up tight and nodded. Indigo had never seen her so determined.

Indigo climbed on to the Moonbear's back. The rhinostriches squawked and shrieked; vials of sprinkles were scattered across the floor and marshmallows poured from giant cracks in the jars.

"Ready?" Indigo said.

Callisto scrunched her eyes tighter and crouched low.

"Three … two … one … FLY!" shouted
Indigo, and with a great leap, Callisto
unfurled her gigantic wings and took to
the air in a SWOOSH OF STARLIGHT.

"You're flying, you're flying!" shouted Indigo, as the Moonbear swept around the cavern, crashing into bottles and jars.

"Let me steer!" shouted Indigo.

Callisto snapped her powerful bear jaws and bit straight through the strawberry laces, sending Quigley and the Explorers bouncing on to the pile of marshmallows below. Callisto crackled through the air like a bolt of lightning.

The cavern door opened again with a SLAM and a crowd of Marsh Gnomes charged in, hollering, with tubes of Dr Gnasher's toothpaste in their arms. They squirted the paste into the air where it fizzed and foamed and freed the Creatures

from the horrible goo.

"Where has Mr Knickerbod gone?" cried Indigo.

Quigley pointed. In all the chaos, Knickerbod and Darling had managed to shimmy along one of the great magic-sucking pipes and were nearly at the door.

"GET THEM!" shouted Madam Grey.

Indigo urged Callisto downwards as she reached out and grabbed two empty bottles.

Then, with a tremendous flap of her wings, Callisto raced towards the churning vat of sauce. Dipping low, Indigo scooped up the sauce and they pelted after Knickerbod and Darling in a flash of white lightning.

As they flew over Knickerbod and Darling, Indigo emptied the bottles. The thick sauce plopped on to their heads.

"ARGGHHHH!" shrieked Knickerbod, bumping into Darling.

They tried to wipe the goo off, but it was no good.

"Callisto … can you land?" Indigo asked breathlessly.

The Moonbear closed her wings and with a great CRASH, she landed, squashing the two prisoners under her bottom.

"Good work, Callisto. We can practise landing later," giggled Indigo.

Indigo and Quigley ran to their parents and gave them GIGANTIC sticky hugs. The gnome toothpaste had done the trick. Everyone was covered in GLOOPY, FIZZY, MINTY foam.

"What do we do with them?" said Indigo, looking furiously at Mr Knickerbod and Ms Darling. Bernhardt was busily tying them together with strawberry laces, just to be safe.

"Lock them up?" signed Quigley.

"Poke them with twigs?" trilled one of the Marsh Gnomes, prodding Mr Knickerbod with his little toasting stick. "He kidnapped us, that one. Said that if the other gnomes told anyone, he'd squash them into wafers."

"We could PICKLE them?" suggested a troll, grinning nastily.

"ROOOOOAAAAAAAR!" suggested the dragon.

"I think that maybe first, we should make them give us our magic back …" said a little voice, and the unicorn stepped forward. "They should give back what they have taken."

Everyone murmured their agreement.

"Yes, of course," said Indigo, rounding on Knickerbod and Darling. "First, you give these Creatures back their magic, then we'll decide what to do with you."

"We are going to need to be able to see," hissed Mr Knickerbod. A Marsh Gnome stepped up and splattered toothpaste in a great dollop on top of the prisoners' heads. Slowly the sauce fizzled away, singeing off their eyebrows in the process.

One by one, the Creatures stepped forward as Knickerbod and Darling miserably uncorked bottle after bottle of stolen magic and poured it into their open mouths. The Creatures seemed to come to life again before their eyes. The unicorn glowed and pranced, the dragon's grey scales shone blue and the fairies fluttered like tiny lanterns as their soft lights returned.

Before they had reached the end of the queue, however, the bottles were empty – the magic had run out.

"There's not enough left! He's used the rest in his horrible ice cream," said a little Marsh Gnome, sadly. The griffin began to cry.

Indigo glanced at her parents and the other Explorers, who looked as crestfallen as she felt.

"Right," said Indigo, suddenly thinking of the world's best plan. "Have any of you heard of our house? 47 Jellybean Crescent?"

The Creatures all mumbled and nodded. "Those of you who haven't got your magic back – and anyone who is hurt – you can come and live with us. I can't be certain it'll work, but if we look after you, help you to recover, your magic might return."

"A fantastic idea," boomed Mr Abernathy, "but we still need to decide what to do with these two." And he pointed crossly at Mr Knickerbod and Ms Darling.

"We can take them to the Explorers' Council, dear," said the Enchantress Cleopatra. "They'll know exactly what to do. I daresay the Elders will find a punishment fitting their crimes."

"Ho, ho! Brilliant idea," chortled Mr Abernathy, his great moustache billowing. "We can drive there in that infernal ice-cream van."

"Fabulous plan," Gazania Atakuma agreed. The Explorers pushed the prisoners out of the cavern and off up the portrait-lined hallway. Indigo could hear Mr Knickerbod yelling all the way.

"This isn't the end! You'll see! Nobody will

stop me! Nobody, do you hear me?"

"Right, well … those of you who want to come with us … we just need to find a GLURK," said Indigo.

"Oh, we can easily find a Glurk." Her mother beamed. "We have lots of fairies here and I'm sure they would find one for us." The fairies glowed with pride and began to swarm. There were a lot of Creatures who wanted to come to Jellybean Crescent and Indigo just knew the house would be ready and waiting to welcome them all.

"You are coming too, aren't you?" Indigo said to the Moonbear, who nodded.

"Oh, yes, I could do with a nice rest
… and somewhere to practise my flying,"
Callisto hummed.

Indigo beamed and turned to Madam Grey,
who was still sitting astride the rhinostrich as
if she had spent her whole life riding magical
Creatures around a deadly jungle.

"Madam Grey, I …" Indigo began.

"Call me EDWINA," said Madam Grey and
then she did something Indigo had never seen
her do. She smiled.

"Are you coming back with us?" said
Indigo, but she thought she already
knew the answer.

"No, Indigo, I am not. I see now what your bear friend meant – people in our world *have* forgotten how to be interesting. Well, not me. I've been boring and beige for too long. This time in the Wilderness has opened my eyes to all that I've been missing. I belong here now. Pebbles and I will be just fine." And she patted the little dog, who, Indigo thought, still looked a bit shell-shocked.

"Well, thank you ... thank you so much for saving us. Look after the Jungliest Jungle for us, won't you?" asked Indigo, smiling.

Madam Grey nodded, smiled and with another yodelling SHRIEK, she called her rhinostrich herd and they galloped out of the cavern, across the hallway, up the twirling staircase and out into the Unknown Wilderness.

-THIRTEEN-

47 JELLYBEAN CRESCENT, AGAIN

The house was the same as ever when Indigo and Quigley arrived home. Unfortunately, though, the Glurk had opened directly into the bowl of the toilet in the downstairs bathroom. Fishkins the purrmaid was hollering from his bathtub about trespassers in his loo.

It took a while for all the Creatures to arrive through the Glurk as there were so many, but finally, Indigo saw her parents climb out of the toilet behind the last Marsh Gnome as the Glurk sealed shut with a wet SPLAT.

Queenie, Olli and Umpf were first to greet
them with bowls of stew and tall glasses of
pink lemonade. The new Creatures were all
found rooms to call their own and before
long it felt like they'd always been there.
IT WAS GOOD TO BE HOME.

THE Daily Waffle

MISSING EXPLORERS FOUND

The mystery disappearance of six Explorers has been solved by none other than Indigo and Quigley Wilde, the adopted children of Philomena and Bertram Wilde.

Two suspects, Mr Clarence Knickerbod, distant relative of the once-great ice cream maker Sir Balthazar Sprinkle, and his accomplice, Ms Elspeth Darling, were brought to the Explorers' Council by some of their victims. Mr Bernhardt Abernathy, the Enchantress Cleopatra, Professor Gazania Atakuma and Miss Bethesda Brolly were seen marching the bound prisoners into the Council building last night. They appear to have travelled there in Knickerbod's giant ice cream van, which has now been seized as evidence.

THE DAILY WAFFLE can now report that Mr Knickerbod and Ms Darling had been running an illegal ice cream parlour from deep within the Jungliest Jungle, stealing magic from its native Creatures for their own gain.

Their evil plot was foiled when Indigo and Quigley Wilde discovered their secret chamber and rescued the Creatures within, along with their parents and the other missing Explorers. It has been reported that a mysterious figure riding a rhinostrich may also have had a part to play in this intriguing tale, but as of yet, THE DAILY WAFFLE has been unable to locate them.

In the days since the arrest of the two suspects, it has been noted that many plants and Creatures have been seen returning to the Jungliest Jungle. THE DAILY WAFFLE is pleased to report that snortlephants, spotty gozzpicklers, unicorns and even a dragon have been sighted in the area for the first time in many months. Mr Knickerbod and Ms Darling stand trial next week.

The ice cream parlour formerly run by Knickerbod has been taken over by a group of Marsh Gnomes who intend to turn the parlour into a marshmallow emporium, ice rink and jazz bar. For details of their grand reopening, turn to page 24.

PRODUCT RECALL

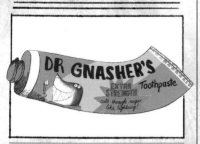

Recall Hotline: 4321672

We are recalling this product from sale due to reports of side effects. After an inspection of the Dr Gnasher factory, it was found that an employee had been accidentally mixing Fireweed extract into the mixture instead of Floss-enhancer. If you have this product, please return to your nearest store for a full refund. Discontinue use immediately. Side effects include: singeing, melting, and uncontrollable hiccups.

Pippa Curnick grew up in rural Essex, UK,
and spent most of her childhood climbing trees,
jumping over ditches and daydreaming in her
treehouse. She studied at Camberwell College of Art
and the University of Derby.
Pippa draws her inspiration from long walks
in the woods, and can often be found
scribbling ideas in her sketchbook.
You can find out more at www.pippacurnick.com.

THIS LITTLE BUG GUY GETS EVERYWHERE.
EACH TIME YOU TURN THE PAGE AND SEE
A PICTURE, SEE IF YOU CAN FIND HIM.